Nicolette

The Raven Siren

Filling the Afterlife from the Underworld:

A FRIEND IN NEED

By

C. S. Woolley

A Mightier Than the Sword UK Publication

Filling the Afterlife from the Underworld:
A Friend in Need
Nicolette Mace: The Raven Siren

By c. s. woolley

Cover design by c. s. woolley
Photography by Jared Drake
A Mightier Than the Sword UK Publication

Paperback Edition

ISBN 9781791300913

To prevent unauthorised copies of this book being made a number of intentional errors have been included.

For Gavin

Nicolette Mace: The Raven Siren -
Filling the Afterlife from the Underworld
Notes from the Case Files of the Raven Siren
A Friend in Need

Contents

The Things I do

Bar fights are not really a common occurrence, even when I'm around. Most people seem to think that violence follows me everywhere I go, but that really isn't the case at all.

I have only been involved in one bar fight in my life, so far, and this was it. Now this was not a simple punch up between a few drunks ending with a few broken bones and both parties being charged with assault.

This was the full Airplane! treatment - and if you don't know what that is, then there is something clearly missing from your life.

It wasn't the best thing to happen in Joe's place, but there was little that I could do to stop people throwing furniture about in every direction, or throwing each other through the portions of the walls where windows had been before the brawl had started.

I was somewhere in the middle of the

main scuffle, but this wasn't my fault. I'd like to make that perfectly clear from the start. I just happened to be in the wrong place at the wrong time.

I managed to fight my way clear of the main knot and escape to the door, but as I reached it, it swung open and I collided with the person who had charged through it.

I looked up to see the last person that I wanted to be running into at this moment in time. It was Inspector Fred Barlow, friend, annoyance and someone that I was currently not on the best of terms with. Behind him was Detective Harry Lee.

"Oh shit," I said and tried to make my way back into the mass of bodies still fighting to escape, but Fred grabbed me by the arm.

"Why is it that you always seem to turn up right in the middle of trouble?" he asked me whilst shaking his head.

"Just lucky I guess," I scowled at him.

"Settle down or I'll be hauling you

all in for disturbing the peace," Harry shouted as a line of men in uniform came through the door to break up the fighting.

Most of the people involved in the brawl separated and started to clear up the mess under the direction of the policemen; the few that refused to stop fighting were placed in cuffs and hauled out of the door.

"You really don't do yourself any favours," Fred said looking at me with disappointment.

"Don't tell me, I have the right to remain silent?" I asked looking up at Fred with defiant eyes.

"I've got no choice," he shrugged as he turned me round and cuffed my hands behind my back.

Harry was having nothing to do with my arrest, he was content to stand on the other side of the bar, overseeing the other policemen.

As the first of the arrestees for the night was dragged past me and out of the bar, Joe Dawson, owner and barman of Joe's, stood up from behind the bar and came over to Fred, protesting my arrest.

This wasn't the best of days. Any day when I see Fred with handcuffs in hand and headed towards me isn't a particularly pleasant one, but I'm getting ahead of myself. Let me take you back to where it all went wrong.

The Call

Today was a rare day; a day when I could relax and I didn't have a care in the world. I was sat behind my desk with my feet up, a cigarette in one hand and a book in the other.

When the phone started to ring, I ignored it and carried on reading. I wasn't in desperate need of work, so there was no having to answer my phone, no having to deal with my neighbours or even the general public.

There was no having to deal with Fred or Harry or even worry about assassins or Kevin Metis destroying my life. Today was a day just for me.

But by the time the phone rang a third time, I was annoyed at the disruptions, so I put my book down, took out a glass and half-filled it with whisky. I took a drag on my cigarette, threw back the contents of the glass and answered the phone.

"Nicolette Mace, the Raven Siren," I

said, my voice more than a little terse.

"Siren, it's Joe," Joe Dawson never called me unless it was urgent.

"Joe, what do you want?" I asked.

"I need your help," he replied. He sounded very shaken as he spoke.

"You need my help?" I asked as I put out my cigarette.

"Yes, but I can't talk about it over the phone, can you meet me at Sal's Café in the next ten minutes?" he asked.

"I'm on my way," I'd never let Joe down before and I didn't intend to now. I made sure that my glass was empty before I grabbed my gun and coat and made my way out of the office.

Like I said, today was a rare day, a day just for me.

It took me less than ten minutes to get to Sal's Café. Joe was sat at a table by the window. His hands were wrapped around a cup of coffee and he was rocking backwards and forwards.

The café was full of people eating breakfast and drinking all manner of hot beverages. I saw Joe straight away and sat down opposite him.

"Damn Joe, you look like hell," I said with sympathy as the waitress made her way over to me.

"What can I get for you?" she asked.

"Tea and the sausage, bacon, eggs, mushrooms, pancakes and hash browns breakfast," I replied without looking at the menu.

"Okay, anything else for him?" she asked me, eyeing Joe with a small amount of concern.

"I think he's good, maybe some water. How much coffee has he had?" I replied quietly.

"Five cups in the last half hour," the waitress told me.

"Yeh, get him some water," I said as I reached over and tried to pry the cup from Joe's hands.

"No!" he yelled, causing everyone in the café to stare. I let go of the cup and held up my hands so Joe could see they were empty.

"Joe, that's nothing in there, let me have it," I said slowly, trying to keep Joe calm after so much caffeine.

"No," he said flatly. He hadn't stopped rocking backwards and forwards since I had arrived. I lowered my hands and sat back in the booth. The rest of the café's occupants went back to their food whilst we waited in silence for my breakfast to arrive.

The waitress came back a few minutes later with my tea and Joe's water.

"Thanks," I said, the waitress nodded at me and then very quickly went off to tend to her other tables, "So you spent twenty minutes drinking coffee before you called me and asked me to come and meet you?" I asked him as I sipped my tea.

"Yes," Joe replied curtly.

"You own a bar, Joe, how much did you have to drink before you came here?" I asked suspiciously.

"Don't know," Joe shrugged.

"How many empty bottles were there?" I asked. I was beginning to get very worried about Joe and what on earth had happened for him to have called on me for help.

"Seven," Joe said after quite a while had passed.

"How many of them were full before you started drinking?" Joe didn't serve beer by the bottle so it was either wine or spirits he'd been drinking. Either way, seven bottles was rather a lot.

"Four," he replied, his eyes fixed on the empty coffee mug.

"Thought you'd given it up a long time ago," I hissed under my breath and resisted the urge to shake my head, "well, that's the end of your liver. I'm surprised you managed to make it here after all that," I joked but Joe didn't react.

I waited for a few minutes to see if he was going to say anything, but when he remained silent, I said,

"Joe, what happened to make you drink?"

"They killed her," Joe's voice was hollow.

"Who killed her? And who is her?" I asked, my brow furrowed. I leaned in towards Joe and had a sinking feeling in the pit of my stomach.

"She's dead. She was just lying there."

Before Joe could say anything else or I could ask any more questions, the waitress came over with my breakfast and put the plate down in front of me.

"Any sauce?" she asked me.

"No, thanks," I replied, I normally would have asked for tomato ketchup, but I was not only distracted by what was going on with Joe but I also thought it best that the waitress didn't come back to table until I knew what had gone on.

"Joe, what happened?" I asked more urgently than before.

"They killed her. She's dead," he repeated.

"Come on, Joe," I urged.

"Her eyes were open and staring, and the blood, so much blood," he was still rocking backwards and forwards as he spoke.

I took out my phone and dialled.

"Hello?" Fred's voice crackled out of the receiver.

"I need you," I said without thinking.

"Oh really?" Fred asked with a slight laugh. It was really not a good time for him to try and flirt with me.

"Fred, I'm serious," I said dryly. I was beginning to think that calling Fred was something of a mistake.

Sweet Siren

I was sat in the police station when Siren called. My name is Inspector Fred Barlow and there is nothing better than a beautiful woman phoning and saying the words "I need you".

I was in the middle of paperwork, but for Siren, I'd drop everything. She didn't sound happy and I could hear what sounded like Joe Dawson in the background babbling away about something.

"Fred, I'm serious," Siren sounded less than impressed.

"So am I," I grinned.

"Fred, this really isn't the time," she sighed.

"What? Not the time for me to tell you -" I began, but Siren cut me off.

"Don't even say it."

"Nic, you know what I am going to say and you know I mean it," I told her. There never seemed to be a good time for me to tell her how I felt, so I had decided that every time we talked was the best time to tell her.

"Fred, this is not the time," she sounded frustrated, but I didn't care.

"When is the time?" I asked, feeling annoyed that it was so easy for her to dismiss my feelings.

"There isn't one," she said quietly.

"I don't think that's true," I sighed.

"You can believe me or not, but right now is not the time," she replied. The door to my office opened and Detective Harry Lee stood in the doorway. He tapped on the glass and I waved him in.

"Who's on the phone?" he asked as he came to perch on the corner of my desk.

"Nic," I told him.

"Hi Siren," he called out.

"Hi Harry," she shouted back and I had to hold the phone away from my ear, "Fred, please will you just listen to me?" she begged.

"Listen to you about what?" I asked as I leant back in my chair.

"Joe is sat with me, and he's seven

sheets to the wind and he's had more caffeine than is good for any human being," she replied.

"Joe's drunk?" I frowned.

"Seven bottles, four of them full."

"Joe's drunk?" I repeated.

"Joe's drunk? The guy who owns a bar and has never had anything to drink as long as I have known him? He's drunk?" Harry asked in disbelief.

"Harry, shut up. Why did he get drunk?" I asked Siren.

"A woman's dead. He keeps repeating over and over about blood and her eyes," Siren explained.

"He does what now?" I asked. Joe was not a man to talk about the grim or the gruesome, so to be talking about a dead woman, blood and her eyes was somewhat out of character.

"Can you and Harry go and check his place? See what's what down there whilst I try and sober him up and get some sense out of him?" she asked me. At least she hadn't been lying about needing me.

"What if we find something that isn't great for Joe?" I asked. I knew how close Siren and Joe were and how protective she was of him.

"I have never asked you to pervert the course of justice and I never will. You find what you find and we take it from there," she said earnestly to me.

"Okay, if you're sure," I agreed.

"I'm sure, I should go, my breakfast is getting cold," Siren said and hung up the phone.

Before she put the phone down I was certain that I could hear Joe repeating,

"She's dead and they killed her."

"Harry, we need to get to Joe's, from what Siren has said it sounds like Joe is in some serious trouble," I said wearily,

"What kind of trouble?" Harry asked as I stood up.

"The kind that gets you locked away for the rest of your life," I shrugged, "What did you come in for?"

"To get away from Turndune, the guy is getting on my last nerve," Harry grinned at me.

"Do you often come in here to get away from people?" I asked with a slight frown.

"Yep, especially when you're out," he admitted.

"I wondered why things kept moving around in here," I laughed.

"Oh, well, that wasn't me. That was Siren," Harry replied.

"What do you mean?" I asked.

"Well, you have a skylight and she knows how to break into this place, you figure it out," Harry patted me on the shoulder, "Come on, let's get going already."

You Got a Friend

When Fred and I got to Joe's Place, nothing seemed to be out of place. My name is Harry Lee, police detective and currently on what I thought was a wild goose chase.

It's not that Joe drinking wasn't strange, but with his underworld dealings, I was surprised that he hadn't witnessed more people being murdered.

After a while you get desensitized to things, and Joe's reaction was not that of someone who was used to seeing death.

From what Fred had told me that Siren had said Joe was traumatised by something. Whether it was because he'd been forced to witness something terrible, drugged or tortured, from the look of the bar, Fred and I were wasting our time.

The bar was all locked up, but Fred had the spare key to the place - the number of times that Siren had been to Joe's for a lock in that Fred had to come and pick her up from, it ended up being easier for him to have his own key.

Inside, everything was as it should be. The chairs were all stacked on the tables, the blinds on the windows were all down, the floor was clean and the bar was wiped down and only the hum of the fridges behind it could be heard.

"Do you think that he drank here?" I frowned as Fred and I made our way around the room. Though nothing seemed out of place from the door, now we were here we might as well check the whole place over properly. It's a matter of pride in one's work - oh and the fact that if we missed anything, Siren would never let us forget it.

"Probably down in the cellar," Fred replied with a sigh.

"Okay, well, I'll start down there then, see what I can find," I replied with a slight shrug.

"Alright, I'll see what I can find in here and then we can check upstairs," Fred said.

"Keep your wits about you," I teased

him as I made my way to the door to the cellar.

"What do you mean by that?" Fred demanded with a furrowed brow.

"I heard what you were saying on the phone," I grinned.

"About what?" Fred tried to play innocent, but I wasn't buying it.

"Were you really going to tell her over the phone?" I asked with exasperation.

"Well, she wouldn't let me tell her to her face," Fred said defensively.

"You've tried?" I asked with surprise, I didn't think that he had it in him to tell Siren that not only did he love her, but that he couldn't live without her and would spend the rest of his life loving her.

"Of course I've tried," Fred shot back angrily.

"What happened?" I asked.

"She held her Beretta right between my eyes and dared me to say it," Fred mumbled and I burst out laughing. I couldn't help it, "It's not funny!" Fred yelled at me.

"Oh, I think you'll find it is," I spluttered as I tried to stop laughing.

"Just because all the women that are part of your life only hang around for three dinners," Fred grumbled.

"That's not fair. It's at least four," I winked.

"Really?" Fred asked wearily. He clearly didn't like how much fun I was having.

"At least I can get women to come out for dinner with me," I shrugged with a grin.

"We've had dinner," Fred pouted.

"No, you haven't, you've eaten together but you've not taken her out to dinner," I sighed.

"Go check the cellar already," Fred said with irritation. I laughed and waved at Fred as I opened the door and went down into the cellar.

I could hear Fred sighing as he moved around the bar, taking his frustration out on some of the furniture that got in his way. I couldn't see anything out of place in the cellar, though I did find where Joe had been drinking. When I made my way back up to the bar, Fred was wrestling the jukebox back into place and was clearly not in a better mood.

"Find anything?" he grunted as he heaved the heavy machine back into place.

"There are a lot of empty bottles down there, way more than seven," I replied. There had been closer to fourteen and signs that someone else had been drinking with Joe.

"You think Joe drank more than he thought?" Fred asked as he straightened up and made his way over to where I was leaning on the bar.

"No, I don't. There's cigarette and cigar butts down there too. Looks like if it was Joe drinking down there then he wasn't drinking alone," I replied.

"That doesn't sound good," Fred huffed.

"You find anything?" I asked.

"Nope, this place is clean. Too

clean. I think someone has been round here and blitzed the place," Fred said as he stood on the opposite side of the bar to me.

"You ready to check upstairs?" I asked cocking my head towards the door that led to Joe's private rooms.

"Yeh. I'm starting to get a bad feeling about this," Fred sighed and followed me.

I took the stairs two at a time, whilst Fred stomped on every step behind me. When we reached the top of the stairs, Fred and I split up so we could search the five rooms that were above the bar. Fred went to check the kitchen and bedroom whilst I went to the bathroom and dining room, with a plan to meet in the middle at the living room and check that over together.

It didn't take much for us to both check the two rooms we had and there was nothing to explain why Joe had gone off the deep end. There was nobody there and no sign that there had been anyone there for some time.

"All clear?" I asked as Fred met me in the corridor.

"Yeh, there's nothing out of the ordinary," Fred sighed and ran his fingers through his hair.

"This is really starting to make my skin crawl," I admitted as we stood in dim light that filtered through the open doorways.

The whole place was too clean and too quiet. One or other is fine, both together normally spells trouble.

"You know, I really don't want to see the living room," Fred said and pressed his lips together so hard, they folded inwards.

"Me neither," I agreed, but I put my hand on the door handle and pushed open the door slowly. Fred stepped into the room first and as I followed we found that it was just as clean as the rest of the bar.

Honestly it left us both feeling confused and I was a little disappointed.

"There's no taste of iron in the air, no smell of death, no cleaning fluids, nothing," Fred half-growled.

"I doesn't even smell of alcohol up here," I said as I clicked my tongue against my teeth. Even though we hadn't found a body, something didn't feel right about this whole situation - and I was pretty sure that it wasn't a wild goose chase anymore.

"Something just isn't right," It was always good when Fred confirmed what I was thinking.

"I know for a fact that this place is never *this* clean," I replied, shaking my head.

"No, from what Nic has said, it's never this clean up here and the bar downstairs is never that clean either," Fred sat down on the couch and leant his head in his hands to think. As I sat there watching Fred, something occurred to me.

"Where is Joe's wife?" I asked.

"What?" Fred looked up at me with a frown.

"Joe's wife, she's sick, right?" I asked as I made my way back into the hallway.

"Yeh," Fred said as he stood up to follow me.

"But she's not in the hospital right now?" I asked as I hurried down the corridor to the bedroom.

"No, Nic said she was let out last week and that Joe was going to be looking after her," Fred called after me as I barrelled into the bedroom. I pulled open wardrobe searching for anything that belonged to Joe's wife as Fred began to rifle through the drawers.

"Her clothes are all still here," I said as I was certain that all the women's clothes in the wardrobe belonged to Joe's wife and not Joe.

"There's jewellery here, books, notes, shoes, it doesn't look like anything is missing," Fred said as he shut the drawers.

"So we're looking at a rear window situation," I sighed as I sat down on the edge of the bed.

"Rear window?" Fred frowned at me.

"Hitchcock, you really need to be more cultured. Everything is here but his wife," I sighed.

"You think that it was her that Joe was talking about?" Fred asked me, though it was pretty obvious to me that it could only be his wife that Joe was babbling about.

"Would seem like the best reason to start drinking if you've never drunk before," I replied as Fred took out his phone and dialled.

"Fred?" Siren's voice came out of the speakerphone.

"Ask Joe where his wife is," Fred instructed her.

"What?" Siren half-shouted down the phone.

"Ask Joe where his wife is," Fred repeated much more calmly and less like he was ordering her.

"He's not replying. I don't even think he can hear me, Fred. You think that he's talking about his wife?" Siren said quietly.

"I don't know, but she isn't here. We're checking the hospitals next, but I'm not holding my breath on finding her there," Fred replied.

"Why would anyone want his wife?" I asked. There were a lot of things you could say about Joe's wife, but she wasn't the most useful or desirable woman ever born.

"I don't know, any ideas, Nic?" Fred asked with frustration.

"Just one," Siren replied and hung up.

Physical

I was sat on the sofa opposite my bed, in the tiny room I was holding up in. It was a motel room of sorts, with just enough privacy to make sure that only the people I wanted to find me could.

I'm known as Ryuu Blade. You don't need to know anything more than that. I was sat in the room cleaning my guns, the parts littering the coffee table alongside my katana and my other assorted weapons.

The floor was littered with takeaway food cartons, some of which were open and I was still eating from, when the door to the room opened and Kevin Metis waltzed in.

"So you're back now?" he asked in a tone that sounded displeased.

"Excuse me?" I asked, putting down the gun barrel I was cleaning and leaning back on the sofa.

"You were gone for a few days. I'm saying you're back," Metis replied in a quieter voice that had lost its demanding edge.

"Yes," I replied, fixing him with a steady stare.

"Where were you?" Metis asked from the doorway. He hadn't moved from there since he closed the door.

"Working," I said, a slight smile curling at the corner of my mouth.

"You work for me," Metis said with annoyance. He was a very territorial creature.

"Not exclusively," I sighed as I picked up the gun barrel and began cleaning it again. I didn't like clingy men and Metis was rapidly becoming exactly that. Clingy men were dull and boring. They were men that got in the way and needed constant validation. They were men that ended up dead.

"You've been taking jobs on the side?" Metis pouted and I shot him a withering glance.

"Yes,"

"I don't want you doing that," Metis came over to where I sat and stood in front of me.

"That's a shame," I replied in an off-hand manner.

"Why?" Metis scowled.

"Because you're going to end up disappointed," I said flatly. The next thing I knew Metis had grabbed me by the wrist, hauled me to my feet and slapped me across the face.

I dropped the gun barrel and responded by kicking Metis in the stomach. He staggered back and dropped to one knee. I didn't give him a chance to recover. I leapt over the coffee table, knocked Metis backwards and pinned him on the ground.

He began to struggle underneath me and it didn't take more than a moment before we were wrestling on the ground, trading blows until Metis had the upper hand and had me pinned.

"I am not the kind of man you want to disappoint," Metis was breathing heavily as he lay on top of me. The exertion had excited him but he was still in control of himself for the moment.

"I am not the kind of woman who

cares," I told him with disinterest.

"I know you were working for Derek Long, I know that you were tempted to fulfil the open contract he has on dear Nicolette's life. If you had done and Siren were dead now, I would be spending the next decade showing you how great my displeasure was and you would see just how I got my well-earned reputation. As it is, she is still alive, so I will only punish you for working for one of my rivals without my consent," Metis whispered in my ear.

"Punishment?" I whispered back. He pulled both my arms up above my head and held them there with one hand; he used his other hand to grip my chin as he kissed me. It wasn't romantic, it was rough, hard and I felt my lip split as he bit my lip before he moved his mouth down my neck, biting as he went.

"You are going to tell me everything you know about what Derek Long is up to and how I can disrupt his business and keep him out of my hair whilst I deal with Siren," Metis murmured as he moved his free hand down my body.

"And what do I get out of it?" I asked, enjoying the physical contact and the change in Metis' attitude.

"You think I don't know what a woman like you wants?" he asked as he brought his lips to hover millimetres above mine.

"No, what do I want?" I asked, looking up at him with great expectation.

"You want money, you want a fierce reputation and you want powerful men on their knees before you," Metis replied.

"And you will give me all of that?" I asked playfully.

"Reputation you already have. Money, well, money is easy," Metis said.

"And powerful men?" I smiled at him for the first time since he had entered my room.

"I'm a powerful man," he breathed as he loosed his grip on my wrist and shifted his weight so that I could slide out from underneath and stand over him.

As I stood there, him knelt at my feet, I tilted his chin upwards so that he was looking up at me. He reached up and grabbed hold of my hips and pulled me towards him. I ran my fingers through his hair as he rested his chin on my stomach.

"And how are you going to punish me?" I asked as pulled his head back by the hair.

"That depends on the information you give me," Metis had a wolfish grin on his face, and he was no less excited now than he had been when he was on top of me.

"You're not going to punish me," I told him firmly.

"No?" he asked, his breath catching in his throat as he struggled to control his composure.

"No, because though you are powerful and dangerous, by letting you slip between my legs, I can get anything I want from you," I told him as I released his hair and stroked him under the chin with one of my fingers.

"Is that so?" Metis asked as I placed my hands on his shoulders and slowly sank to my knees so that I was straddling him. I could feel him pressing against me and slowly began to grind my hips against him.

"Yes. I'll give you the information you want and in return, you'll do exactly what I want," I whispered as Metis let out a slight moan.

"And what's that?" he asked. I let him kiss me before I pushed him down to the floor.

"You're going to let me have some fun," I said.

Doctor, Doctor

As Harry and I had failed to find anything at Joe's Place and the fact that Joe's wife was missing, the hospital was the next place for us to visit.

There hospital was always busy, as most hospitals seem to be. When we walked through the automatic doors and up to the reception desk there was a doctor leaning on the desk that the nurse behind it was trying to flirt with.

"You think she will understand that if we can't find his wife here then we have to take him in for questioning?" Harry asked me in a low voice as we walked over to the desk.

"I think she knows we'll have to, but I don't think for one second she will be anything close to understanding about it," I replied with a heavy sigh.

"She's been through all this enough times," Harry shrugged.

"And when in any one of those times has she been reasonable about being arrested or seeing people being taken in for questioning?" I asked, shaking my head.

"I see your point," Harry allowed as he reached the desk and he grinned at the nurse.

"Can I help you gentlemen?" she asked. The name tag on her uniform read *Nancy*.

"Detective Lee, Inspector Barlow, we're wondering if you can tell us if there is a Mrs. Dawson that has been brought into the hospital in the last twelve hours, Nancy," Harry always was the first to talk to women he thought were attractive.

"Mrs. Jessica Dawson?" the doctor asked as he turned towards us both.

"Yes, doctor?" I asked.

"Doctor Lees, Mark Lees," the doctor introduced himself and offered me his hand, "Mrs. Dawson is a patient of mine; she's being treated for an aggressive leiomyosarcoma. It's a rare form of cancer," the doctor explained.

"Has she been admitted in the last few hours for any reason?" I asked as Harry continued to make eyes at the nurse.

"Not that I am aware of, but I'm just her surgeon, not an oncologist. If you give me ten minutes I'll be able to check for you. Nancy, I'm sure you have patients waiting," the doctor clearly didn't like competition as far as flirting with nurses went.

"Yes, doctor," she said as the doctor sat behind the desk and began to search the records for us.

A cup of coffee too much

As I sat waiting in the café to hear back from Fred and Harry, I was becoming even more concerned about Joe.

He had stopped responding to everything around him and was still babbling whilst he rocked backwards and forwards.

The café was getting busier as time ticked away, and more people were casting Joe weird looks as they passed by. I was sat with tea in one hand and my phone in the other.

"Joe, I need you to focus. I need you to listen to my voice and I need you to start making sense," I sighed as I tried in vain to get through to him, "Fred and Harry are trying to help you, but they can't if you don't give me straight answers."

Joe looked up at me from his coffee cup, as though he had only just realised I was there.

"Joe, where is your wife?" I hissed under my breath. There were a lot of people in the café and I was sure at least half of them very trying to listen to what we were saying.

"I don't know," Joe said quietly.

"You said, 'she's dead'," I told him.

"Yes," he agreed as he broke down into tears and dropped the cup on the table, spilling coffee everywhere.

"Joe, is Jessica dead?" I asked gently.

"Yes," he sobbed.

"Okay," I said; breathing heavily as the waitress came over to clear up the mess. She looked at me with a grim expression before she walked away.

"Joe, how did she die?" I asked when I was sure the waitress was out of earshot. But Joe didn't answer; he just started to cry harder. I was so preoccupied with my crying friend that I didn't notice the door to the café opening and Fred and Harry walking through it.

"Joseph Dawson," Harry said gravely as he stood beside the table, Fred hanging back a little.

"Don't you dare, Harry," I warned him as I stood up to look him squarely in the eye.

"Nic, please, don't make this any harder than it already is," Fred said, trying to get me to back away from Harry.

"You're under arrest," Harry continued as if I wasn't there.

"No," I said as I drew my Berettas and aimed them at Harry and Fred.

"Nic, put the guns down," Fred sounded like he was in no mood to deal with drama, but I was now in full scene mode. I wasn't going to let them arrest Joe without a bit of a fight.

"No. You aren't arresting him," I was more than a little adamant about it.

"It's okay," Joe croaked as he managed to stop crying.

"No, it isn't. You called me for help and I am going to help and part of that help is not letting Morecambe and Wise arrest you," I said hotly.

"Siren, please out those down. I don't want to get shot today," Harry gave me a withering look. But before I could reply, gunfire erupted outside the café.

The windows disintegrated in a hail of broken glass. Joe, Harry and Fred dropped to hide behind the booth as I began to fire back at where I thought the shots were coming from.

Other people in the café all dove for cover, screaming as they went down. I emptied both clips and ducked behind one of the booth seats to reload.

"You could help!" I yelled at Fred and Harry.

"How?!" Fred shouted back.

"Shoot at something!" I cried with exasperation.

"With what?" Harry asked as more bullets sprayed into the café.

"You aren't armed?" I asked in disbelief.

"When are we ever armed?!" Fred demanded.

"I thought after everything that's happened so far this morning, you'd have come slightly more prepared," I replied, shaking my head.

"We brought handcuffs," Harry shrugged.

"Not at all helpful right now, we're not in your bedroom, Harry," I said sweetly.

"Funny!" Harry said sarcastically.

"Do me a favour?" I asked them both.

"Does it involve shooting?" Fred asked as a bullet snapped a little too close to his head for comfort.

"No," I said, rolling my eyes.

"Okay," Fred agreed.

"Take Joe home, make sure he is okay. I have a feeling I know who is behind all this and where Jessica is," I replied chewing my bottom lip.

I stood up and began firing again as I slowly walked across the diner. I couldn't see who I was aiming at as the sun was behind them and shining in my eyes, but as bullets started to graze my arms, torso, and legs, I knew I wasn't far off my mark.

As I reached the door of the diner, I kicked it open and stepped out into the street. The sun was finally out of my eyes, so I could see a handful of figures piling into a car and the screech of tyres as it drove off.

I followed the car as best as I could on foot, firing at it as I went. It was soon out of range, so I went back to the café. Several of the patrons and the waitress that had been serving Joe and I were lying dead on the floor.

Harry had his phone out and was dialling whilst Fred was checking over people with injuries. Joe was curled up on the floor under one of tables and it seemed best to leave him there for now.

"Hello? Yes, this is Detective Harry Lee, we need an ambulance at Sal's Café. There's been a shooting, multiple victims, unknown assailants," Harry said as he was connected, "No, it wasn't Siren, she chased them off," Harry explained after a brief pause, "They ruined her breakfast."

He really does think he's funny.

"You've got to give it to her; she doesn't half pull off the angry, psychotic bitch act well," Fred smiled to himself.

"I'm standing right here," I said as I holstered my guns.

"That's assuming it's an act," Joe croaked from under the table.

"Still standing right here," I sighed.

"You finally snapped out of it?" Fred asked as he walked over to where Joe was hiding.

"My wife is dead, Fred, I doubt I'll ever snap out of it," Joe replied meekly. Harry had hung up the phone and was checking the dead bodies.

"The ambulances are on their way, we should do what we can," he said to me.

"Who is the worst?" I asked as I looked around the room and Fred pointed to a girl that had been shot in the chest. One of the other café patrons had his hands over the wounds, trying to stop the bleeding.

"How is she doing?" Fred asked as he coaxed Joe out from under the table.

"Not good, I'll stay here and deal

with all this with Siren; you take Joe home and see what else he can tell you," Harry said from my shoulder.

"Alright, I'll meet you back at the station," Fred replied and escorted Joe out of the back of the café as the sound of sirens filled the air.

I waited until Harry's attention was focused on the people in the café before I slipped out the front and started walking as the rain started.

The Usual Suspects

It was best that I wasn't at the café to be questioned by the police that would be filing in there. Most of them were not my friends and would think any reason was good enough to lock me away for a few days.

Ordinarily it would be somewhat inconvenient, but on a day like today; it would be the difference between Joe being arrested for murder and sent away to prison forever, and finding the real killer.

The rain seemed oddly appropriate as it became heavier and I pulled up my collar to keep the rain from seeping down inside my coat.

When a car full of thugs pull up at a diner in broad daylight and shoot the place up, not long after a certain bar owner's wife is reported to be dead, there are only three people that spring to mind as being responsible.

Surprisingly, Danny MacDonald features quite high on the list of the usual suspects, so rather than going to meet with either of my arch-nemeses, I thought I'd check in with Danny.

Danny was sat behind his desk when I walked through the door. His office didn't look all that different to mine; only his office was falling apart.

His office was old and worn with a door that had a broken pane of glass. There was a musty atmosphere in the room and it was always dark.

Behind a rickety old door to one side of the room, a disgusting toilet could be seen, and if this place had ever been cleaned, it was before I was born.

Danny had an L-shaped wooden desk which had an old, cracked and faded leather chair behind it, which Danny sat in.

There was a low bookcase that had more dust and cobwebs in it than books. The windows were behind were Danny was sat and so dirty that no light could filter through them. The only light in the room came from the broken panes that neighbourhood children had thrown stone through.

Danny was smoking a cigar and reading

through a stack of old files when I walked in.

"Niccy, my girl, what a pleasant surprise," Danny smiled at me as he looked me up and down. Danny was a very creepy guy.

"Being around you is never pleasant, Danny," I sneered and made sure that I kept my distance from him.

"Then why do you spend so much time coming to visit with me?" Danny asked as he put the file he was reading down on the desk.

"It's not visiting, Danny, it's an interrogation. If you weren't the creepiest man alive, you'd know the difference," I replied with a scowl.

"If you were better at interrogation, there wouldn't be so much confusion," Danny chuckled in reply.

"Stunning that you never had a career as a stand-up comic, truly, shocking," I shot back dryly, but I knew I needed to keep the conversation going in the direction I wanted and not give Danny the chance to steer it away from the point of my visit, "I've had an interesting morning. Got a call from Joe that a woman was dead and then a bunch of thugs shot up the diner that I was meeting with him at. Anything you want to tell me?" I asked bluntly as I stood before Danny with my arms folded.

There wasn't much point trying to be subtle with Danny. He had a nasty habit of being slippery at every possible opportunity. He was supposed to be a private investigator, just like my father was, but really he was just another underworld minion working for the highest bidder.

I would say he sold his soul, but I'm pretty sure he never had one to begin with. My biggest problem with Danny though was that he had known me since I was a little girl and there wasn't any situation where he took me seriously.

Trying to be tough really got me nowhere, but equally standing in front of him with my arms folded and expecting an answer didn't seem to be doing me much good either.

As soon as I asked the question, Danny burst out laughing and leant back in his chair to look at me with the steady gaze he had that made my skin crawl.

"You really do seem to go looking for trouble, don't you?" Danny asked me as he leered.

"Trouble seems to find me," I replied with a sneer.

"I don't know what you think I could possibly know about any of this, Niccy, my girl. I'm just a simple private investigator trying to make a living," Danny replied with the cocky arrogance I'd come to expect from him.

"Simple I would agree with. It takes a less than average mind to ally yourself with the scum that pay your bills," I retorted and continued to glare at Danny.

"You have a nasty little tongue there, Niccy, my girl. Be careful or someone might come along and cut it out. There are lots of nasty men out there and it isn't very safe for women who go about crossing them. It isn't safe for the wives of men that cross them," Danny chuckled to himself.

"Where is Joe's wife?" I snapped. The bastard was just toying with me and I had had enough.

"Joe who?" Danny smirked.

It was at this point I may have lost my temper just a little bit, and Danny was reminded why it wasn't a good idea to piss off slightly unhinged women that carry guns.

Getting Joe back on his feet

Having already paid a visit to Joe's Place, I knew that it didn't need to be tidied before it opened, but I did need to make sure that Joe was in a fit condition to actually serve people without breaking down or being completely plastered.

The best thing for Joe was to open the bar and try to keep his mind and hands busy whilst Harry and I found out what was going on. I was pretty certain that Siren didn't really want to work with us, as normal, she'd do her thing and we'd do ours and meet somewhere close to the end of it all. The we'd compare notes and either arrest the criminal responsible or we'd arrest Siren for shooting the criminal who was responsible.

Whichever way it turned out, Harry and I'd be arresting someone, so all this wouldn't hurt our numbers.

Joe's binge earlier in the day didn't seem to have drained his stores too badly, so he still had plenty of stock to see him through the night without having to reorder.

Joe staggered between the tables, knocking a few of the chairs down as he went. With all the coffee, gunfire and other traumas, I was surprised that he hadn't passed out before now. But there wasn't much keeping him awake now.

Before he reached the bar, he had fallen face first onto the floor. He groaned slightly but his breathing changed from that of a drunk struggling to get up to that of a man that was fast asleep.

I waited for a few minutes until I was certain that he was out, then I picked him up, threw him over my shoulder and carried him up to his bed.

I got a glass of water and put it on the bedside table. I also got a bucket and put that by the bed, just in case.

When I was sure that Joe was settled, I went back down to the bar and took all of the chairs and stools down from the tables and the bar so that at least some of the preparation for opening the place was done.

I went to the back door and made sure it was locked and also checked the cellar again.

There was something about the bar that had me on edge. I couldn't put my finger on what was wrong, but I just knew something was.

It felt like I was being watched by an unseen force, the same kind of feeling I got when I walked through my apartment door after Siren had broken in and moved all my furniture so that it was out of place by an inch.

It's a niggly little thing, but all I could do to make sure Joe was safe was to check the place was locked up, that no one was hiding in wait in the bar and try and find out what in the hell had happened to Joe's wife.

Station-Bound

The situation at the café was a mess and as there was a considerable amount of overkill involved and my presence at the scene, pretty much everyone assumed that Siren had something to do with it.

But, as she had scarped pretty quickly after the end of the blazing gun battle, she wasn't around so no one could say that she was definitely involved.

I left the forensic team in their Tyvek suits to go over the scene and had a niggling thought that Siren had left something at the crime scene that would link her to the gun fight.

There wasn't much that I could do at the diner. I made sure that the body of the waitress was carried out in a dignified fashion, and that the constables had kept the press back behind the tape.

With them guarding the scene and my statement given to the responding officers, the only thing I could do was head back to the station.

I knew that Fred would be heading there once he had sorted out the bar for Joe and made sure he was safe in the joint.

We both knew that there was something seriously wrong at the bar and with Joe, but without evidence or even a statement from Joe about what actually happened there was nothing we could do.

It seemed fairly obvious to me that the she Joe kept mumbling about was his wife. So we could safely assume that she was dead, however that was hard to prove without a body.

The next thing we needed to work out was who the "they" was. With the amount of underworld bosses that Joe was under the thumb of, it could have been any number of people.

I didn't think that Jarndice or his gang of thugs had anything to do with it. Jarndice may be a gang leader but he has rules and one of them is that women and children do not get brutally murdered, especially those who are sick, dying and have no part in any criminal enterprise.

Sykes and the Snake Devils were a possibility, but I didn't think that they were smart enough to think of so thoroughly cleaning a potential crime scene after they had been there.

No, whoever it was, they were clever, they were organised and they were sending a message.

By the time I had come to this realisation, I had pulled up at station to find Fred was waiting for me by the door.

"Thought it was best we went in together," he smiled at me wryly.

"You know people are going to assume Siren did the shooting," I replied.

"Yeh, I know. It would be surprising if she wasn't responsible for 50% of the repairs the city has to pay out for every month," Fred sighed.

We made our way into the bullpen and went to Fred's office. As he outranked me, he had his own walls and a door that could be used to keep out the unwanted interruptions of cops like Ross Turndune, Richard Ellis and Gary Rogers.

“So what do you think?” Fred asked as he flopped into his chair and I shut the door.

“Well I doubt Joe killed his wife, but someone clearly has,” I replied

“Though where the murder took place and where the body is now are unknown. So hard to make that stick,” Fred sighed.

“Fred, I know that you are trying to think of this in terms of arrests and getting a conviction, but right now can we please just think in the abstract. Otherwise we’re never going to get anywhere, Siren will find the guy, kill them and then get caught because she’s way too brazen for her own good; and she doesn’t know the meaning of subtlety or tact,” I asked pointedly. My normal good humour had been somewhat eroded by Siren running off and having to deal with the first responders at the diner.

“All right then, you carry on,” Fred said with a wave of his hand as he leaned back in his chair.

“There were cigar butts and

cigarette butts in the cellar, and Siren darted off as soon as you and Joe were out of the diner, which leads me to think of one person," I said, ignoring Fred's flippant attitude.

Before I could name the man that had sprung to my mind, and most probably Fred's, the phone on Fred's desk started ringing.

"Hello, Inspector Fred Barlow," Fred said as he picked it up.

I waited patiently as Fred listened to whoever was on the other end of the phone.

"Right, I see. Thank you for calling," Fred sighed as he put the phone down.

"What is it?" I asked with a frown.

"Siren tried to kill him," Fred said shaking his head.

"Who did she try and kill?" I asked, not at all following Fred's train of thought.

"Who were you about to name?" Fred asked with exasperation.

"Danny? Siren tried to kill Danny?" I spluttered.

"According to the complaint made by Danny, Siren tried to throw him out of the window in his office," Fred said, trying to sound disapproving, but I knew how close he had come to throwing Danny out of that window before. So it was hard for me not to detect a certain amount of glee in his voice.

"Shame she didn't succeed," I muttered.

"She ran out of there when the police showed up after concerned neighbours called them," Fred continued, ignoring me.

"Concerned neighbours? In Danny's neighbourhood? Sounds like a set-up to me," I snorted.

"Considering the officers were on scene to see Siren pushing his head through the glass of the window - definite set-up," Fred growled.

"So, what are we going to do?" I asked.

"We need to find Siren and bring her

in to find out what Danny told her. Danny is at the hospital now, but we both know that is Ellis or Turndune get to her first, she's going to be locked up and out of our reach," Fred replied as he stood up and took his coat off the back of his chair.

"Well, there is only one place that Siren is going to go to after all that," I grinned.

"Joe's Place it is. We should take some uniforms with us. Make a big show about arresting her," Fred said thoughtfully.

"That's not why you want to take uniform," I said, shaking my head.

"Of course it is," Fred said innocently.

"Don't bullshit me; you think Siren has gone back to Joe's to protect him. Someone tried to kill him at the diner and you want to protect her. We turn up with uniform, then any would be assassin is going to think twice. Even Ryuu Blade," I replied curtly.

"Alright, we'll take uniform to pull

her ass out of the fire because she's in over her head and I don't want her dead," Fred allowed.

"Just marry her already," I jibbed as I followed Fred out of the door.

Set Fire to the Third Bar

After dealing with Danny I needed a drink. Fred would probably say I needed anger management classes, but I'm quite happy with how I currently deal with my rage.

Danny had pushed my buttons a little too much and after he alluded to knowing exactly what had happened to Joe's wife. Pushing his head through a window was probably not the best way to try and get information out of him, but the police were already outside when I did, so I had to get out of there rather sharpish.

I'm sure that Danny would have talked after a few minutes of being held out of the window, but with the threat of arrest I really didn't have that kind of time.

As I darted away from Danny's taking the back stairs and diving through one or two of the lower floor apartment windows to avoid the police coming up, I managed to slip away and gave myself time to think about what had happened there.

For the police to be on scene so quickly, someone had to have tipped them off. The only way anyone would have known to tip off the police was if they had followed me from Sal's café.

The more I thought about it, the more I was convinced that someone had been following me all day - or at least since I met with Joe. It was possible that whoever the stalker was had been following Joe since he left his bar, and then followed me to Danny's after Fred took Joe home.

From what Danny had not said, there were only two people that could be behind this - Kevin Metis and Derek Long. No one keeps their lips so tightly sealed as those being paid by criminal kingpins.

The involvement of either man did not feel me with joy, but at least I would know what I was dealing with. The only person that could tell me for certain was Joe, so my visit to his bar was twofold - getting the drink I needed so desperately and finding out which of my archenemies was trying to kill people in my life today.

I opened the door to the bar and found it was as busy as always with the usual mix of men avoiding going home, people engaged in illegal activities, the small group of drinkers that had wandered in, oblivious to what was going on around them, and a few thugs looking for trouble once they'd had enough to drink.

I made my way through the maze of tables to the bar where Joe was stood, cleaning glasses behind it as though the events of the morning had never happened. The bar was open from midday and rarely emptied until closing time.

As I walked over to him, a woman dressed in tight jeans, dancing near the jukebox caught my eye. There was a small group of young men watching her, and she had been clearly trying to catch their eye with how she was parading herself. But there was something very familiar about the woman that I couldn't put my finger on.

"What's shaking, Siren? Been a while since I last saw you," Joe greeted me with a slight quiver in his voice.

It may seem like he was trying to be sarcastic since it was barely a few hours since we had last parted ways, but there were ways of talking in public.

As I wasn't the law and wasn't the criminal scum that gave people in the city a hard time, it wasn't always safe to associate with me; especially for someone like Joe.

Anyone in the bar could have been sent there to keep an eye on Joe and by greeting me like this, it told me that it was best to not mention anything that had happened during the course of the day until we were alone.

So my questions would have to wait, but my drinking didn't have to.

"Been busy, Joe," I replied with a forced sigh.

"Busy looking for answers at the bottom of whisky bottles in your office? You know that you should really talk to someone about what is going on in that head of yours," Joe said. As ironic as it may seem to an outside observer, this was Joe's way of talking about himself when he couldn't be explicit.

"I don't do talking about feelings, Joe. You know that," I snorted as I sat at the bar and casually cast my eyes about the place.

"What can I get for you?" Joe asked. He was shaking slightly, something I took for the effects of so much caffeine and alcohol on his body, but I had to admit that I was impressed by how well he was functioning.

"The usual, and any information you have on what Kevin Metis is up to now he is free of his cage," I said in an offhand manner. I was taking a stab at one of the two names I thought were responsible for this mess and seeing what I turned up.

Joe picked up a glass and a bottle of single malt without saying a word, put the glass on the bar and poured out the whisky.

"You're asking about Kevin Metis?" a voice asked from over my shoulder. It was a voice I knew all too well and it told me that I had found my target.

"That's none of your business," I replied without turning round. I picked up the glass off the bar and slowly began to sip the perfectly aged scotch. A moment later, I found bar stool spun round so that I was face to face with Bob Davies, one of Kevin Metis' more dangerous peons.

He swiped his hand at me, but he wasn't looking to hit me. Instead he knocked by glass out of my hand, sending whisky flying across the bar.

I looked down at the empty glass that had smashed on the floor and the wasted golden liquid.

"Joe, another whisky on the baboon if you please," I sighed wearily and rolled my shoulders. Trouble was brewing and I needed to make sure I was loose enough for the fight that was headed my way.

"Baboon? Who are you calling a baboon?" Bob demanded as he towered over me, reeking of body odour, cheap cigarettes and halitosis.

"The jumped up pile of walking lard that just ruined my drink," I said calmly.

"He said that you had a mouth on you, but not much to back it up," Bob sneered. I had made it my business to know everyone that worked for both Kevin Metis and Derek Long, even if they didn't know me - I knew them.

"Who said?" I asked coolly, looking him in the eye for the first time.

"Kevin Metis. He sends his regards," Bob laughed. Behind Bob there were seven men at a table all watching the exchange. At the mention of Kevin Metis' name, all of them stood up. Two of the men with Joey and Louis Davies, Bob's younger brothers, the other five I didn't know. So either they were new to the organisation or they were thugs that had been hired for the occasion.

"Oh, how quaint, hired thugs. I was expecting a highly trained and overpaid assassin," I said with more sarcasm than was necessary.

So clearly this was not my fault.

The seven men all lunged at me, but

seven men diving for one target gets messy, especially when the target dives over the top of the bar so that they collide with it and some of the other patrons that were sat drinking.

By the time I put my head back over the bar, furniture was flying in all directions and nearly everyone in the bar had been drawn into the fracas.

I tried to make my way out of the bar without getting drawn into any of the fighting, but if you've ever tried to leave a fight that consumes a whole bar, you'll know it's just not that easy. I got dragged into the central mass of bodies that were wrestling, punching, biting, eye gouging - it was a no holds barred free for all.

I finally managed to drag myself out of the fighting and made my way to the door.

As I reached it, the door swung open and this is pretty much where you came in.

"Why is it that you always seem to turn up right in the middle of trouble?" Fred asked me whilst shaking his head.

"Just lucky I guess," I scowled at him.

"Settle down or I'll be hauling you all in for disturbing the peace," Harry shouted as a line of men in uniform came through the door to break up the fighting.

Most of the people involved in the brawl separated and started to clear up the mess under the direction of the policemen; the few that refused to stop fighting were placed in cuffs and hauled out of the door.

"You really don't do yourself any favours," Fred said looking at me with disappointment.

"Don't tell me, I have the right to remain silent?" I asked looking up at Fred with defiant eyes.

"I've got no choice," he shrugged as he turned me round and cuffed my hands behind my back.

Joe had been hiding from the danger behind the bar, but now he made his way over to where Fred was tightening the cuffs around my wrists, and doing his best to appear not to be enjoying himself.

"Fred, for once, this isn't her fault," Joe protested, but it did no good.

"Not the reason she's being arrested Joe," Fred replied shortly as he spun me round and looked down at me with a severe expression.

"What do you mean? Has this got anything to do with Jessica?" Joe asked worriedly. Jessica was the name of Joe's wife and it was the first time that he'd actually confirmed that Jessica was the she that he had been talking about earlier in the day.

"You know I can't tell you that," Fred replied flatly.

"Wait, what are you arresting me for?" I frowned up at Fred.

"Siren, there are witnesses that claim you tried to murder Danny MacDoanld," Harry sighed.

"Excuse me?" I scoffed.

"We've got no choice," Fred whispered in my ear and I did my best to stop my body from shivering.

"Wait just one minute. Do either of

you actually believe that I tried to murder Danny?" I demanded.

Fred and Harry looked at each other, but didn't say a word.

"Oh well, that's just great. The two people who claim to be my friends think I'm a murderer," I half-shouted.

"Can you blame us?" Harry asked me with a helpless look on his face.

"What?" I was really starting to lose my temper now.

"Siren, you lose your temper and resort to violence more quickly than anyone else I know and with all the threats you make, and the body count you leave in your wake - murdering a man that you can't stand with very little prompting is not that far to leap," Harry replied shortly.

"Detective Lee, if I could slap you right now, it would shatter every one of your perfectly whitened teeth," I snarled through gritted teeth, "And you!" I turned my attention to Fred who had been suspiciously silent so far, "You, you honestly think that I would do something as low as murder to get rid of Danny? If I wanted Danny dead, I would have dragged him to the police station, shot him between the eyes and let you arrest me on the spot," my voice was barely below screaming now.

There was a murderous look in my eyes as Fred gently placed his hand on my shoulder and tried to steer me out of the door. I shook free of his hand and glared at Fred,

"Don't touch me. I'd expect such stupid behaviour from Turndune and Ellis, but not from either of you. I thought you were both better than that, more intelligent, but I guess you're nothing but two stupid -" I was going to continue my tirade but Fred squared up to me, matching my stare and cutting me off.

"If you finish that sentence, I'll make sure that you live to regret it," Fred said in a low voice that gave me chills. I stared back at him for a few minutes, my chest moving up and down as I struggled to control myself.

From the looks on Joe and Harry's

faces, I was pretty sure they thought I wanted to kill Fred, when right now, the opposite was true.

I didn't finish my sentence; instead I broke eye contact with Fred and walked towards the door without his assistance. Fred followed close behind.

We walked out to where his car was waiting and he put me in the back before closing the door.

Sleight of Hand

Watching Fred and Siren fight is never a pleasant experience, and in the last few minutes I honestly couldn't tell you whether Siren wanted to take Fred to bed or take his head off.

Joe and I had followed the pair out of the door and watched Fred put Siren in the back of his car.

"I'm sorry about that, Joe," I said as I shook his hand.

"You brought all those men down just to arrest her?" Joe asked in wonderment.

"Fred thought we might need some form of back up," I shrugged.

"I don't think I've ever seen her that angry before," Joe marvelled as Fred got into the front of the car.

"No, me neither," I admitted.

"You okay?" Joe asked.

"Not really," I replied with a careless smile, "She's right, attempted murder really isn't her style and deep down, I don't think either of us believe it, but then again -" I sighed and shook my head.

"Then again, the witnesses tell you different," Joe hung his head and closed his eyes.

"Yeh," I agreed.

"You sure they aren't lying?" Joe looked at me sideways with a gleam of hope in his eye.

"Nope, but we don't have a choice," I said firmly.

"So you keep saying," Joe replied dryly.

"You think we do?" I asked with surprise. For a man that had been as drunk as he was a few hours ago, I was impressed with how he was handling himself.

"I wouldn't know. But Siren has always been there when we've needed her, and right now, neither of you seem to be there for her. Why would she kill Danny anyway?" Joe asked.

"He was here earlier wasn't he?" I asked in a low voice, and Joe slowly nodded, "And Jessica is dead?" Joe nodded more and tried his best not to cry, "Well looks like Siren found the connection between Danny and Jessica's death and went to do something about it," I finished.

"So why would she kill him?" Joe demanded.

I shrugged. I knew what Joe was driving at. If Siren wanted to get revenge on Joe's behalf then she'd be much more likely to maim him, put a few rounds through ball and socket joints and then turn the bastard in to the police. Killing him flat out was really more of an assassin's thing. And Siren really hates assassins.

"I see. Well, do yourselves a favour. Make sure that Larry doesn't find out about this, otherwise you'll find yourselves having to deal with more than just Siren being angry," Joe warned before he disappeared back inside.

I walked over to the car where Fred was patiently waiting for me, and slipped into the passenger seat.

I put on my seat belt as Fred

started the engine. We pulled away from the bar in silence.

I glanced in the rear view mirror to see Bob, Louis and Joey Davies stood outside of Joe's Place watching us leave. Each of them had smug grins on their faces. The car turned the corner and the bar disappeared out of sight.

"Okay we're clear," I sighed with relief.

"Then get these things off me," Siren said as she thrust her hands towards me. I reached into Fred's pocket and pulled out the key to the cuffs.

It took me a few seconds to unlock them and Siren rubbed her wrists in a dramatic fashion when they were off.

"Next time, try not to be so convincing," Fred sighed as he looked at Siren in the rear view mirror. He sounded quite hurt. I knew that he hated arguing with Siren, but there were times when she really hit close to the bone with her verbal jibes.

"You told me I had to sell it, after

all, this won't work if Metis suspects you know anything," Siren replied.

Once the call had come through about Siren trying to kill Danny, I had gone to check the call logs to see what I could find out. The call had come from a burner phone, but upon listening to the call, I recognised the voice as belonging to Bob Davies.

From there it wasn't too much of a leap to discover that Metis was behind at least some of what was going on. I'd texted Siren and left it up to her to discover whether it was Metis that was behind Jessica's death.

"You think he'll believe we're convinced of your guilt?" I asked as I sat properly in my chair and watched the road ahead.

"Why not?" Siren asked as she lounged about in the back of the car.

"Because it's us and you," Fred replied quietly. Clearly Fred needed an apology from Siren at the very least before he was going to feel better.

"We'll find out soon enough. If it hasn't worked, we haven't lost anything for trying," Siren replied with a shrug.

"You could have pulled some of your punches, you know," Fred huffed.

"I was handcuffed, I couldn't hit you," Siren said with a raised eyebrow.

"Verbal punches," Fred sighed.

"Fred, I kinda think she was," I said slowly. I knew how cold Siren could be and as upset as Fred was with her for the things she said, I knew she could have said much worse.

"You think I held back?" Siren asked with amusement.

"Definitely," I replied firmly

"Oh?" Siren laughed.

"You know that slapping me isn't exactly a threat, you know more than enough about both of us to come out with way worse things," I replied as I looked out of the window.

"Like what?" Siren asked innocently.

"Well for a start, you could have attacked Fred physically when he stood that close to you - knee to the groin or head butting him," I said in an off-hand manner.

"You think me holding back will mean Metis doesn't believe you're arresting me?" Siren asked seriously.

"Maybe, like you said, we'll see," I shrugged.

"Well for what it's worth, I'm grateful you didn't attack me," Fred smiled.

The Grind

It didn't take Fred and Harry long to incarcerate me in the cells at the police station. I'd spent plenty of nights there before, so it wasn't the most unpleasant experience. There was no one else being held for the moment, so it was fairly quiet and the duty sergeant was completely disinterested in me.

So I lay down on the bed in the cell and gazed up at the ceiling, thinking about what could have possibly happened to Jessica.

There wasn't a doubt in my mind that Joe's wife was dead now and that Kevin Metis was behind it, but what I really didn't understand was why.

As much of a bastard as Metis was, he wasn't a man to murder a sick woman for no reason. Amongst other things, he was using her for leverage over Joe, so killing her just didn't make any sense.

I'd spent about two hours mulling things over when my musings were interrupted by a voice calling out to me through the metal grate in the door.

"Well, well, well, all alone in a dark damp cell. What a way to spend an afternoon. You must be so terribly bored in there Siren," it was Kevin Metis in the flesh.

His voice made my skin crawl, and though I had been expecting the visit, I was by no means any less nervous being unarmed and only having a metal door between us.

"No, I actually have brain cells so lying back and thinking is quite an enjoyable experience. I'd say you should try it, but you're short some of the necessary equipment," I replied as calmly as I could, though I was shaking slightly. I was glad that he couldn't see in from where he was standing, but I was beginning to feel very exposed as I lay there.

"How quaint, though I know how much fun your tortured mind is. Maybe we can pass an evening together, exploring the depths of it," Metis said slowly. I wanted to scream and scratch at the walls to escape but whilst the door was closed and locked, I was safe from him.

"Or we could grind out enemies to talcum powder with a sledge hammer, but gee, we did that last night. Wait a minute, not that was definitely you and it wasn't your enemies, it was a man's sick wife," I half-shouted as I sat up, watching the door as I kept my back to the door.

"How sweet and naïve you are. They really are your most alluring qualities you know. Your youth is responsible for it I suppose, but it really is quite irresistible," Metis said as he placed his hand on the door with a loud crash.

I shuddered and bit my lip to stop myself from whimpering. I wasn't going to give him the satisfaction of hearing that I was afraid.

"You're a sick bastard," I sneered.

"Sick? No. Perverted? Quite possibly. Corrupted? Almost certainly. I know that when we first met, Siren, I crawled up inside your head. That night I took away your innocence, I claimed it as my own and whilst I possess it, I will always dominate your mind. But I have yet to finish what I have started with you. Your father was a weak man and your sister, she was no fun at all. But you, Nicolette, you are something special. Before I am done with you, I will have you begging me for more," Metis continued.

"I will never beg you for anything," I replied coldly.

"Oh, you will beg me for more just as Mrs. Dawson begged for her life. It really was quite pathetic to see her begging like that, but then again, she shouldn't have tried to cross me that way," Metis sighed.

"What do you mean, crossed you?" I asked. I was starting to feel a little light-headed. I wanted to lie down and sleep but only a few minutes before I hadn't been anywhere close to tired.

"Oh Nicolette, Jessica wasn't the sweet and innocent woman you imagine her to be. She was working for me in a far greater capacity than Joe was. Did you know that

Jessica hated Joe? She married him for his money. Working for me, she hoped to earn enough money to leave him and pay her medical costs so that she could get better and reclaim a life far greater than the one she had been living. But there is a problem with people like that. They are invaluable, but they don't want to be criminals forever. They're only interested in making a lot of money very quickly and then moving on. That isn't very good for business. The truth is, Jessica would have gotten well at any time, if only she had stopped taking the medication she was prescribed," Metis laughed.

"You bastard, you were making her ill? You were draining every penny out of Joe and slowly killing his wife?" I spat. I had to shake my head to keep myself from falling asleep. My eyes were getting heavy and my speech had started to slur slightly.

"It was practical. Keeping her ill meant she worked for me and was completely under my control. It also kept Joe very amiable and pliable as well. All-in-all, it worked out very well for me," Metis said in an off-hand manner. I was so tired now that I couldn't respond.

"Ah, I take it by your silence that the drugs are finally taking effect. Drugs do seem to take an awfully long time to affect you, but it's no matter. The duty sergeant has stepped out for a few hours and no one will be coming to check on you until the morning," Metis said with glee

"But why shoot at Joe?" I spluttered. I knew I was in trouble. I wasn't sure how he had managed it, but the water in the bottle by my bed was the only thing I had eaten or drunk since I been at Joe's Place. Whatever drug Metis had used, it had to be in that.

"Oh, that wasn't Joe being shot at; he's never been anything but a willing peon. No, the little hail of bullets was for your benefit. Nothing gets your attention more acutely than a little hot lead," Metis laughed. I started to cough and fell from the bed to the floor. I was barely conscious as I heard the key turn in the lock, the door open and the footsteps of Kevin Metis approaching.

"Well, little colt, it's time to have some fun," he said and I passed out.

Harry's unexpected guest

Fred and I left Siren at the station for the night. There wasn't any real reason for either of us to stay there. Metis wasn't going to try and get to her in a prison cell, and at least she would be out of the way and safe for once.

It was only mid-afternoon by the time Fred and I finished out shift, but it had been a long enough day that all I wanted to do was to go home to bed. And by go home to bed, I meant alone.

I opened the door to my apartment and made my way through to the bedroom. I took off my jacket and tie, throwing them and my trousers onto the chair that sat by the door. I jumped in the shower very quickly, and by the time I came out I was almost asleep on my feet.

I crawled into bed and drifted off as soon as my damp head hit the pillow. When I woke up it was dark, but despite the lack of light, my whole body told me I wasn't alone anymore.

"Who's there?" I asked. I've always thought the idea of saying that to the darkness is rather stupid, but it turns out I couldn't be original or even witty when I found myself faced with a need to say it.

"I'm impressed you could tell I was here," a woman's voice I didn't recognise drifted out of the black.

"What kind of Lothario would I be if I couldn't tell when there was a woman in my bedroom?" I replied as I sat up and reached for the light.

"I wouldn't turn that on if I were you," the woman warned and I felt her hand grab my wrist. Her grip was firm, but her skin was surprisingly soft.

"Who are you?" I asked as I withdrew my arm.

"I won't say anything as clichéd as 'a friend', mainly because that simply isn't true. I am a friend to no one and there is one man who needs reminding of that fact. That is why I am here," the woman replied.

"That doesn't tell me who you are," I

said slowly, feeling the hairs on the back of my neck standing on end. There was something familiar about the woman that I couldn't place.

I was beginning to get the feeling of **déjà vu as I sat there, but it wasn't until I felt the woman sliding her legs over me, so that she was straddling me, that I realised who she was.**

The scent of her skin came back to me in a flash, and I immediately tried to throw her off, but she was overwhelming strong and I couldn't shift her.

"Ryuu Blade, here to kill me?" I asked as I tried to struggle against her.

"Glad to see our last encounter left an impression," she chuckled in my ear.

"That doesn't answer me question," I said and gave up trying to fight her.

"I already told you, I am here because a man needs reminding of the fact that I belong to no one and that I am nobody's friend," Blade replied.

"And how does pinning me to my bed accomplish that?" I asked as coolly as I

could. In truth I was enjoying having this dangerous woman holding onto my wrists as her body pressed against mine.

"Oh, it doesn't. But I am about to ask you for a favour of sorts, so there needs to be some form of exchange. You're well-known for you insatiable appetites and I decided that it would be the best thing to offer you," Blade replied and I felt her tongue slowly licking my ear.

I let out an involuntary moan as I felt her lips on my neck and she pushed her hips against me.

"I take it you're agreeable?" she asked and I felt lace brush against my bare chest. She was wearing a mask on her face made from lace, something I assumed she wore just in case any light filtered into the room whilst she was there.

"That depends on the favour," I replied with heavy breathing as I tried to resist accepting what she offered without knowing what she wanted in return.

"Kevin Metis has become too possessive. He thinks he can dictate who I work for, when I work and what I do with the rest of my time. That is unacceptable. But never fear, I'm not asking you to do anything to him that you wouldn't want to do. You have been trying to find out what happened to Mrs. Dawson, correct?" Blade began.

"Correct," I replied as I tried to shift my hips away from hers.

"She is dead, Metis murdered her. She was providing him with a number of prescription drugs that were necessary for his criminal enterprises. Metis discovered that she was in talks with the Snake Devils to provide them with the drugs instead of him. He's not a man that allows his employees to walk away from him, or indeed betray him," Blade continued.

"So he had her killed?" I asked as I closed my eyes and tried to think of mundane things.

"No, well, he had Danny McDonald take her life, but he was in the room and he made her husband watch. He then took her body from the bar and had it hidden in one of the derelict houses he owns close to the docklands. They're scheduled for demolition in nine months and when they are finally torn down, there are a lot of skeletons that are going to be found," Blade explained.

"And why are you telling me this?" I asked with confusion.

"I want him arrested, charged and convicted of murder - amongst other things. Just a reminder that I will do what I please, no matter who it annoys and who it hurts," Blade replied.

"And where is this derelict house?" I asked as she started to grind her hips against mine.

"I will give you the address after you accept the exchange," Blade said and licked my chest.

"Agreed," I said, unable to resist the woman any longer. What she was asking was what I wanted anyway and there was something irresistible about sharing my bed with a woman that could kill me without a second thought or any guilt afterwards.

She let go of my wrists and I reached out to grab her hips. The moment I did, I felt the silk garter belt she was wearing, and aside from the lace mask and stockings on the belt, she wore nothing else.

If I were a gentleman I would use that as an excuse to not divulge to you what happened between those sheets for the two hours I spent enjoying my time with her, however, we know that isn't the case.

I still won't tell you the sordid details of what we did as firstly, as pleasurable as the experience was I am ashamed of myself for it. After all, she was contracted to kill one of my best friends and I felt like I had betrayed both Fred and Siren by bedding the assassin.

I also don't want you telling Siren all the details. It will be bad enough if she just finds out that I was willing to sleep with the woman trying to kill her.

The two hours passed far too quickly, but by the end of it I could barely move and Blade was lying beside me, letting out a number of contented noises.

"An acceptable exchange?" I asked as I slowly stroked her skin, feeling the beads of sweat that lay on it break beneath my fingers.

"Your reputation does not do you justice," she breathed and then laughed to herself.

"What?" I asked.

"Nothing," she replied and I felt her roll off the bed.

"What about the address?" I asked.

"It is on a piece of paper on the nightstand," she replied.

I reached for the lamp switch and flicked on the light. Beside the bed there was a slip of paper with an address scribbled on it.

I looked up and caught sight of her scantily clad body from the back and had to fight the urge to drag her back into my bed.

"Thank you, I'd ask you to stay, but this was a transaction that I think you would consider complete," I said as I picked up the piece of paper.

"There is one other piece of information I have to exchange, that is if you are interested?" she said coyly.

"How long an exchange do you suggest?" I asked as I climbed out of the bed and stood behind her.

"Until dawn," she replied. I grab hold of her and bit her hard on the neck. I didn't care what information she had to exchange, I was just happy to be able to enjoy her for a few more hours.

When I woke up the next morning, Blade was gone and I was left with memories of a night that I could never share with anyone. I sighed contentedly and looked at the nightstand. She had placed the address back by the lamp along with another note.

The second scrap of only had five words written on it.

He has Siren there too.

It took reading the piece of paper and couple of times for the meaning of the words to sink in. Suddenly I was very awake and reached for my phone. I dialled quickly and waited for an answer.

"Hello?" Fred groggily asked on the other end of the line.

"We've got trouble. Metis has Siren," I replied.

What's a girl to do?

When I opened my eyes I was not in the police station anymore. From the light coming in through the window, it had to be early morning.

I wasn't really sure where I was and my head was pounding from whatever it was that Metis had drugged me with. I had been asleep for a very long time and was very glad that I was a) waking up at all and b) that no part of my body was aching.

The room I was in was barely a room. The building it was in seemed to be falling down, but there was a large bed in it that looked like it was new. The headboard was made from metal railings and I didn't like the look of the handcuffs that lay around two of the bars.

I was tied up and sat on a chair facing the bed, but otherwise the room was empty. I knew I wouldn't have long until Metis came to finish what he had started a few years before. I tried to stand up but found that I wasn't just tied up, I was tied to the chair.

It was also at this moment that I realised I wasn't wearing any clothes. I should have felt cold in the room but the drugs in my system were numbing my senses and even slowing my mind still.

The door to the room opened and Kevin Metis loomed in the doorway.

"Now, little colt, by the time I am through with you, you'll be begging me for more," he grinned and shut the door behind him.

Handcuffs without a safety word

After Harry called me, it didn't take me five minutes to get dressed and get out the door. Harry was waiting for me by the curb outside his apartment block as I pulled up as well.

I felt so stupid. We'd both been convinced that though Siren might have come across Metis whilst she was locked in the cells for the night, he wouldn't be able to do anything to her.

We had both been naïve enough to believe that there wasn't a level of the police that his corruption hadn't infiltrated and that he wasn't bold enough to kidnap Siren from custody.

I felt sick to my stomach as I drove. The address that Harry had was easy enough to find. I didn't know how he had found out about it or how he knew that Metis had Siren, but right now I didn't care, and he wasn't volunteering the information either.

I wanted to bring back up with us, or at least have it meet us there, but Harry pointed out that if Metis could take Siren out of the cells without fear of reprisals then we couldn't trust anybody but the two of us to see her safely home again.

Though we still wanted to help Joe find some justice, this case was no longer about helping him. It was all about saving Siren.

We pulled up outside of the derelict row of houses and were both surprised to find that there was no one positioned outside as a lookout.

The door to the house was unlocked and there was no one inside on the ground floor either. It was beginning to feel like a trap when it occurred to me that Metis had brought Siren here because he felt safe in this condemned property.

He didn't need anyone to protect him because no one would ever dream that these old buildings that barely managed to stay up would be hiding the body of a murdered woman and be the site where another was being held prisoner.

Jessica's body wasn't hard to find.

It was lying, wrapped in plastic sheeting, in the front room of the house. Harry took charge of the body whilst I went to find Siren.

I couldn't hear anything whilst I was downstairs but as I climbed the stairs I could make out muffled screaming that was barely audible.

As I reached the top of the stairs, I heard Metis' voice.

"You are a stubborn little bitch, aren't you? But I will break you. I have all the time in the world to make you give me what I want," he said.

I followed the sound of his voice to a closed door. I kicked it open to see Siren handcuffed to the headboard of a large bed. She had been stripped and been badly beaten, but Metis was still fully clothed. There were a number of weapons that lay on the bed from whips to a baseball bat.

None of them looked like they had been used yet, but Metis' knuckles were cut and bruised, but in a far better condition than Siren's face.

I had never been angrier in my life than I was at that moment. I launched myself across the room and started to pummel Metis as I pinned him to the floor.

I was so lost to my rage I couldn't hear Siren's voice calling out to me. I couldn't hear Harry running up the stairs. I couldn't hear him yelling at me. The first thing I knew of him being in the room was when Harry pulled me off Metis.

"I'm not finished yet," I yelled.

"Go see to Siren. She needs you," Harry told me firmly and stood between Metis and I until I made my way over to the bed to free Siren.

Harry read Metis his rights as the man laughed, pulling him from the room.

"Fred, give me the keys. I'll take Jessica and this trash to the station and come back for you," Harry said. I fished in my pocket and threw the keys to Harry.

The handcuffs holding Siren were not standard issue and had a release catch on them. It didn't take a moment for me to release her. I took off my jacket and put around her shoulders so that she could cover up.

She sat on the bed, perfectly still, not saying a word, until she heard the engine of my car start and drive away.

The moment that she was sure that Metis was gone she burst into tears and threw herself into my arms.

"It's okay, Nic, you're safe now," I soothed as I stroked her hair and let her cry.

The Things I did

I was in hospital for three days after Fred saved me from Metis. I had several bad bruises and a few broken ribs, but mostly I needed the space to feel safe.

Fred came to see me every day, but I didn't feel much like talking to him. Metis was remanded without bail and Fred has been promoted to Detective Inspector before I was released from hospital.

Fred and Harry both came to collect me and see me home, though they didn't stay long.

It wasn't often that I had days like this, days that were just for me.

I decided I couldn't stay in my office or apartment for long as I needed to be outside. I went for a walk and couldn't shake the feeling that I was being followed.

I tried to stay calm as I walked but the anxiety that I was being followed and that I would end up in Metis' hands again became so overwhelming I just had to get home.

When I got back to my apartment, I found there was a single rose waiting for me on the door mat. The sight of it terrified me and I stepped over it, locking my office door once I slammed it behind me.

I almost ran through my office to my apartment and locked myself in. I sat on the middle of my bed and tried to convince myself I was safe.

I sat there for hours doing nothing but repeating, "Metis is in prison, he can't hurt me," over and over again.

The sound of someone trying to open my office door caused me to jump. I sat frozen as I listened to the sound of the door banging against the doorframe.

"Nic? Are you okay? It's Fred. Let me in," Fred's voice called through the door. I felt relief flood over me.

I slowly climbed off my bed, unlocked my apartment, made my way across to the office door and opened it.

Fred was stood with a worried expression on his face. He was dressed in an open collar shirt and trousers that he only ever wore when he was trying to impress women.

"What do you want?" I asked in a small voice.

"To take you out to dinner. You've had a rough time in the last few days. Let me take your mind off it," Fred grinned at me.

"No, thanks," I said and tried to close the door. Fred stuck his door between it and the frame.

"I'm not leaving you alone. You're clearly upset," Fred said as he forced his way into my apartment.

I didn't know what to say to him, I could only stand there and look at him with a helpless expression on my face.

"Please, I just want to stay here and stay away from people," I said when I managed to find my voice.

Fred frowned at me and sighed.

"Then you aren't staying here," he said.

"Didn't you just hear me?" I asked.

"I did, but I also know when you're letting Metis crawl into your head and control you. You know that is what he wants, and I won't let him win. You're going to come back to my place. You can stay there for as long as you like. I'll sleep in the guest room and you can have my bed. You'll be safe there. I have better locks and my building has a doorman," Fred said as he walked through to my apartment and began to pack a bag for me.

I stood in the doorway and watched Fred packing.

"And what if I say no?" I asked.

"If you were going to say no, you would have done so already. You've never been one to mince your words or hold back your opinion," Fred smiled at me.

"You'll have to stop trying to save me some time," I sighed and sat down on the bed next to my bag that Fred was piling my clothes into.

"No, I won't," he said firmly.

"And why not?" I asked.

"Because Nicolette, no matter how

much you try and fight it, you can't change how much I love you. And I am going to spend the rest of my life being there to save you. Whether you like it or not," Fred said.

"Well whadaya know, I was wrong," I smiled.

"Wrong about what?" Fred asked as he zipped my bag closed.

"There was a good time," I replied.

Also by the same author

Nicolette Mace: The Raven Siren

Medusa
Siren's Call
Shadow
A Shot in the Dark
From Out of the Ashes
The Murder of Michael Hollingsworth
The Case of Mrs. Weldon
Hunting the Priest Killer
Manhunt
A Friend in Need
Murder in the First
Sabrina
Filling the Afterlife from the Underworld: Volume 1
Filling the Afterlife from the Underworld: Volume 2
Filling the Afterlife from the Underworld: Volume 3
Filling the Afterlife from the Underworld: Volume 4
Derek Long Saga
Lily & Rose Saga

The Children of Snotingas

WYRD
HILD

The Mysteries of Stickleback Hollow

A Thief in Stickleback Hollow
All Hallows' Eve in Stickleback Hollow
Mr. Daniel Cooper of Stickleback Hollow
The Day the Circus came to Stickleback Hollow
A Bonfire Surprise in Stickleback Hollow
Tinker, Tailor, Soldier, Die
12 Days of Christmas in Stickleback Hollow

Poetry

Standing by the Watchtower: Volume 1
Standing by the Watchtower: Volume 2
Indie Visible: Volume 1

Chronicles of Celadmore

Rising Empire: Part 1

Rising Empire: Part 2

Rising Empire: Part 3

Shroud of Darkness

Lady of Fire

End of Days

When Darkness Falls

The Children of Ribe

FATE

WAR

WIFRITH

DOUBT

SKÅNE

SHIPWRECKED

FEAR

HOME

TREASON

Box Sets

Rising Empire Trilogy

Shroud of Darkness Trilogy

The Arm Rings of Yngvar Collection

Beginnings

The Kevin Metis Saga

Shakespeare Simplified

Merchant of Venice

Merchant of Venice Workbook

Merchant of Venice Teacher's Guide

Much Ado About Nothing

For further information on any of these books please visit:

www.mightierthanthesworduk.com

Books Adapted by C.S. Woolley for Foxton Books

Level 1 400 Headwords

The Wizard of Oz by L. Frank Baum

The Adventures of Huckleberry Finn by Mark Twain

The Adventure of the Speckled Band by Arthur Conan Doyle

Anne of Green Gables by L. Maud Montgomery

Dracula by Bram Stoker

The Prisoner of Zenda by Anthony Hope

The Lost World by Arthur Conan Doyle

Level 2 600 Headwords

Moby Dick by Herman Melville

Gulliver's Travels by Jonathan Swift

Alice in Wonderland by Lewis Carroll

Sleepy Hollow by Washington Irving

Treasure Island by Robert Louis Stevenson

Around the World in Eighty Days by Jules Verne

Robinson Crusoe by Daniel Defoe

Level 3 900 Headwords

The Three Musketeers by Alexandre Dumas

Pocahontas by Charles Dudley Warner

Oliver Twist by Charles Dickens

Frankenstein by Mary Shelly

Journey to the Centre of the Earth by Jules Verne

Call of the Wild by Jack London

Level 4 1300 Headwords

The Count of Monte Cristo

The Merchant of Venice

The Railway Children

Jane Eyre

Level 5 1700 Headwords

The Thirty Nine Steps

David Copperfield

Great Expectations

Twenty Thousand Leagues under the Sea

For more information visit

http://www.foxtonbooks.co.uk

38619777R00068

Printed in Great Britain
by Amazon